Franny's Father is a Feminist

Text © 2018 by Rhonda Leet
Illustrations © 2018 by Megan Walker

Published by POW!
a division of powerHouse Packaging & Supply, Inc.
32 Adams Street, Brooklyn, NY 11201-1021
info@powkidsbooks.com • www.powkidsbooks.com
www.powerHouseBooks.com • www.powerHousePackaging.com

Printed and bound by Asia Pacific Offset

Library of Congress Control Number: 2017963832

ISBN: 978-1-57687-873-6

10 9 8 7 6 5 4 3 2 1

Printed in China

FRANNY'S FATHER IS A FEMINIST

WRITTEN BY
RHONDA LEET

ILLUSTRATED BY
MEGAN WALKER

POW!

BROOKLYN, NY

This is Franny.

This is Franny's father.
Franny's father is a feminist.

He knows that girls can do anything boys can do,
and raises Franny to believe she deserves all the same rights,
freedoms, and opportunities that he has.

It's simple, really.

When Franny's father was a child, he and his sister did chores around the house.

His parents assigned him mowing the lawn and taking out the trash, while his sister did the dishes and helped with laundry.

His sister mowed the whole lawn
in no time flat.

Franny's father was impressed.
He had always loved the smell of fresh laundry anyway.

When Franny was little,
she loved to sort all the tools
from the workbench
in the garage.

Franny's father
taught her all
their names
and also how
to use them.

Soon, Franny could take her bicycle apart
and put it right back together, all by herself

...they've since moved to larger vehicles.

On weekends when he isn't working,
Franny's father takes her fishing.
Franny baits her own hook,
and doesn't even gag a bit!

When Franny catches
more fish than her father,
he tells her she reminds him
of his sister, when she was a little girl.

When the fish aren't biting,
Franny plays in the mud,
catching frogs.

She proudly leaves a ring
of dirt in the tub.

"Girls should be able to do
anything the boys do,"

Franny's father sighs,
and grabs a sponge.

This is Franny's mother.
She has an important job.

When Franny's mother
leaves for work before
Franny is even out of bed,
Franny's father helps her
get ready for school.

He is an expert
hair braider, and knows
all the coolest styles.
But he always lets Franny
pick out her own clothes.

"Just be yourself."

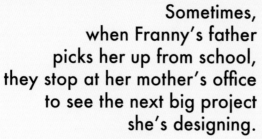

Sometimes, when Franny's father picks her up from school, they stop at her mother's office to see the next big project she's designing.

Franny feels excited when she sees her mother test the latest computer programs. She lets Franny push buttons to make things move on the screen.

On the way home, Franny asks,

"Whose job is more important,
Mom's or yours?"

Franny's father smiles.

"We both share the most important job in the world,
and that's raising you."

Franny participates in many after-school activities.
Franny's father is very supportive.

He is proud of Franny when she helps a teammate score the winning goal at her hockey game.

Franny's father also enjoys
watching her perform in ballet recitals.

Sometimes
he can be
a little TOO
supportive.

After homework time, Franny and her parents love to watch movies together.

When Franny's father
tears up, she hands him a tissue.
Franny knows her dad cries, and that's okay.

Franny's friends love slumber parties at her house.

Her father tells them campfire stories
in their backyard.

Between his favorite ghost stories, Franny's father
slips in tales of historic women
while stoking the fire.

He tells them about Claire Marie Hodges, who in 1918 became the first female park ranger for the National Parks.

And Sally Ride, who was the first
American woman to fly in space.

"One more story before bed," Franny always pleads.

So he tells them of more brave young women, like Ruby Bridges, the girl who broke down racial barriers between segregated elementary schools in 1960.

And Malala Yousafsai, who today is paving the way for girls to be able to attend school all around the world.

Franny and her friends are grateful they already are able to learn in school.

When times are tough,
Franny's father teaches her
that you always have to stand up
for what matters to you most.

Sometimes they make signs.